Little Joe's Horse Race

by Andy Blackford

Illustrated by Tim Archbold

Franklin Watts
338 Euston Road
London
NW1 3BH

Franklin Watts Australia
Level 17/207 Kent Street
Sydney
NSW 2000

A CIP catalogue record for this book is available
from the British Library.

ISBN 978 1 4451 1613 6 (hbk)
ISBN 978 1 4451 1619 8 (pbk)

Series Editor: Jackie Hamley
Series Advisor: Catherine Glavina
Series Designer: Peter Scoulding

Printed in China

Franklin Watts is a divison of
Hachette Children's Books,
an Hachette UK company.
www.hachette.co.uk

The school pantomime was *Cinderella*. Everyone wanted to be in it. Especially Little Joe.

Little Joe wanted to be
Prince Charming. His aunt
used to be an actor.
She tried to help him.

"Oh Cinderella! Will this dainty little slipper fit your pretty foot?"

"It's no good!" complained Little Joe. "Princes are big and strong. I'm far too small!"

"Then you must act taller!" his aunt told him. "Push your chest out! Make your voice tall!"

At the audition, Little Joe tried acting bigger.

"MARRY ME, CINDERELLA!"

he screamed.

But everyone seemed
to like Hector better
than Little Joe.

A letter came from school. Little Joe had a part in the play – as the back end of Prince Charming's horse.

"Never mind," said his best friend Josh. "Guess who's the front end? Me!

We'll be the best

pantomime horse ever!"

"The best ever!" said Joe.

Little Joe and Josh
practised every day,
rain, snow or shine.

They ran and ran – and then they ran some more.

And when they were bored with running, they learned how to jump.

One day, when they went out to practise as usual, there were crowds of people in their field.

They found themselves
mixed up with the real
horses at the beginning
of a big race.

And then they were off!

As soon as Little Joe and Josh realised they were in a race, they ran faster than ever before!

With one last burst,
Little Joe and Josh shot
past the leading horse
to win the race.

The Mayor presented
the boys with their prize.
And Little Joe was an
even bigger star than
Prince Charming!

Puzzle 1

Put these pictures in the correct order.
Now tell the story in your own words.
How short can you make the story?

fed up   sad

excited

bored   happy

nervous

Choose the words which best describe the characters. Can you think of any more? Pretend to be one of the characters!

Answers

Puzzle 1

The correct order is:

1f, 2d, 3b, 4e, 5c, 6a

Puzzle 2

Little Joe   The correct words are fed up, sad.

The incorrect word is excited.

Josh   The correct word is happy.

The incorrect words are bored, nervous.

Look out for more Leapfrog stories:

For details of all our titles go to: www.franklinwatts.co.uk

*hardback